Flip and Flop

Flip and Flop

Dawn Apperley

SCHOLASTIC INC.

New York Toronto London Auckland Sydney
Mexico City New Delhi Hong Kong Buenos Aires

"**Wheeeeee!**" said Flip.

"Look at me! I can stand on one leg."

"Me too!" spluttered Flop. "I can do it too!"

But he couldn't, and toppled
slowly over into the snow.

Flip was five. Flop was two.
Whatever Flip did, Flop did too.

"I'm making a snow penguin," said Flip.
"Me too!" said Flop.

"I'm in my secret hideout," said Flip.
"Me too," said Flop.
In fact, whatever Flip did, Flop did too.

Flip and Flop played a made-up game
called boomba. They jumped into
the snow, bouncing on their bottoms.
"Boomba!" shouted Flip.
"Boomba!" shouted Flop.

Flop loved playing boomba with Flip.
He could play it forever . . .

but sometimes Flip wanted
to play other games.

One day Flip was on the
play slope, playing slip-slide
with his friend Hip.
Flop waddled over.
"Let's play boomba!" said Flop excitedly.

Flip loved Flop. Flop loved Flip. But sometimes Flip thought his little brother was a pest.

"No!" said Flip. "I want to play slip-slide with Hip, not boomba with you. No way!"

Flop felt sad. He shuffled away.

Flop waddled and shuffled,
shuffled and waddled,
up and down,
around and around,
in and out . . .

until he had wandered
far, far away from Flip.

Flop found a new play slope and started to play boomba alone.
"Boomba!" shouted Flop, and fell down. He started to cry.
"Boomba is no fun on my own," sniffled Flop. "It is boring and cold."

At the top of the slope,
someone was watching him.

A little bear came sliding down.

"My name is Hop. Who are you?"
said the little bear.
"I'm Flop," said Flop, grinning. "Do you
want to play boomba with me?"
"Yes," said Hop with a
big smile.

Together they jumped into the snow,
bouncing on their bottoms.
"Boomba!" shouted Flop and Hop
as loudly as they could.
They were having a really good time.

"My brother didn't want to play with me today," said Flop.
"Mine didn't either," said Hop.
"I'm happy I played with you," said Flop.
"Me too," said Hop.

Soon it was time to go home. The two friends skipped back to the play slope.

At the play slope Flip and Hip were bored with playing slip-slide. They looked gloomy.

"Flip, this is my friend Hop,"
said Flop proudly.
"And he's my baby brother!" said Hip.
"Let's all play together," said Flip.
"And make up a new game," added Flop.

Flip, Flop, Hip, and Hop invented
a new game called slip-slide-boomba.
They whizzed, slipped, slid, jumped,
and, all together, shouted:

"Boomba!"

ISBN 0-439-47146-X

18 17 16 15 14   10 11 12 13/0

Printed in the U.S.A.   40

First Scholastic paperback printing, November 2002

Dawn Apperley reserves the moral right to be identified as the author and illustrator of this work.

The text of this book is set in 26-point Providence-infant. The illustrations are watercolor.